ANNIE'S FAIR-WEATHER FRIEND

ADVENTURES
From
The Book of Virtues ™

FRIENDSHIP

Adapted by
Shelagh Canning

Illustrated by
Davis Henry

Simon Spotlight

Based on the best-selling *The Children's Book of Virtues* by William J. Bennett

Based on the television series *Adventures from The Book of Virtues*™,
adapted from *The Book of Virtues* by William J. Bennett, and
produced by PorchLight Entertainment, in association with KCET/Los Angeles.
Executive Producers: Bruce D. Johnson and William T. Baumann

Simon Spotlight
An imprint of Simon & Schuster
Children's Publishing Division
1230 Avenue of the Americas
New York, NY 10020

Book design by RunKid Productions/LA

The text of this book was set in 14-point Century Book.

Printed and bound in the United States of America

10 9 8 7 6 5 4 3 2 1

Library of Congress Cataloging-in-Publication Data
Canning, Shelagh.
Friendship: Annie's fair-weather friend / adapted by Shelagh Canning; illustrated by Davis Henry—
p.   cm.—(Adventures from the book of virtues)
Summary: When she learns that the most popular girl at school was just pretending to be her friend, Annie is upset until Plato,
the buffalo, tells the story of a young Indian named Waukewa, who is a true friend to an injured eagle.
[1. Friendship—Fiction. 2. Conduct of life—Fiction. 3. Storytelling—Fiction.] I. Book of virtues. II. Title.
III. Series: Canning, Shelagh. Adventures from the book of virtues. PZ7.C1712Fr 1997
[E]—DC21
96-37541
CIP
AC

ISBN 0-689-81279-5 (pbk.)

CIGNA

A Business of Caring.
CIGNA is a proud supporter of public television and
Adventures from The Book of Virtues.™

WEB SITE www.pbs.org/adventures

As soon as Annie Redfeather stepped off the school bus, Sarah West, the most popular girl in the fifth grade, rushed over to her. "Your father has a canoe, right?" Sarah asked. "Does he let you use it?"

Shocked, but flattered by Sarah's interest, Annie nodded. "Great!" Sarah exclaimed. "A bunch of kids are going canoeing Saturday. Would you like to be my partner?"

"Sure! Come by my mom's bakery after school, and we'll make plans!" said Annie.

Later that afternoon Annie and Sarah shared some cookies from Annie's mother's bakery. Her father's canoe was next to the back door.

"Gee," said Sarah when she saw the canoe, "it's kind of . . . old!"

"But it's a great canoe!" Annie said.

"Well . . . I guess it will have to do," said Sarah. "This is my chance to impress Bobby Draper!"

"Wasn't that the girl who left you stranded at the library last week?" Mrs. Redfeather asked Annie after Sarah went home.

"Well, yes, but that was just a misunderstanding," Annie said. "Everything's okay now. We're really good friends."

Before dinner, Annie decided to hike to Plato's Peak. She couldn't wait to tell her friends there about Sarah.

Annie had not gone far when she heard someone calling her name. "Annie, wait!" cried Sarah. "Boy, am I glad I ran into you! Listen, I've changed my mind about the canoe trip," Sarah explained, flashing her easy smile. "I'm going with Ashley instead. Her parents just got this cool new canoe. I really can't let Bobby Draper see me in some funky *antique* canoe. You understand, don't you?"

"I guess so," said Annie. "But who am I supposed to go with?"
Sarah just waved and rode away.

When Annie arrived at Plato's Peak, she told her friends about Sarah and the canoe trip. "I really believed she wanted to be my friend," Annie said.

"Not to worry, Annie," said Socrates the bobcat, called Sock by his friends. "You've got us!"

"It's not the same," Annie said. "Sarah is so popular—so cool."

"What are we?" asked Aristotle the prairie dog, Ari for short, "Chopped liver?"

Sarah's friend Zach Nichols explained to Plato the buffalo that Sarah was the kind of girl who used people for her own advantage.

"That's not the way it is at all!" Annie cried indignantly.

Plato thought for a while. "She sounds like a fair-weather friend," he said finally.

"It's not what you *have* that makes a friendship," added Aurora the hawk. "It's what you *give*."

"That's what a young Native American boy, Waukewa, discovered," said Plato.

"Walk? Walk where?" asked Sock, who had dozed off for a minute.

"Storytime, Socko!" called Ari. He was carrying Plato's ancient book of stories of honor and good deeds.

Waukewa's Eagle

Waukewa and his tribe were great hunters and fishermen. One day he and his father were hunting near a mountainside. Waukewa's father was teaching him how to spear fish in the river when they were interrupted by the anguished cry of a bird.

Waukewa ran toward the noise and found a young eagle that had fallen from its nest.

His father examined the bird. "This wing is broken. You must put the eagle out of its misery," he told his son as he went back to the river. "It will be one less thief to steal our fish."

When he was alone, Waukewa pointed his bow and arrow at the eagle. The frightened bird began to shake. Waukewa felt so sorry for the helpless creature, he lowered his arrow. "I won't hurt you," Waukewa said. "I can't do as my father has asked."

Then Waukewa gently carried the eagle home. First he bathed its wing in warm water. Then he made a nest of ferns and grasses.

The boy's mother watched. "Your father will not be pleased," she said as she bound the bird's wing with soft cloth. "But I am. You have a gentle spirit."

"What is this?" Waukewa's father's voice boomed angrily when he returned. "You have disobeyed me, Waukewa! I will have to get rid of the eagle myself!"

The boy stepped in front of the nest and grabbed his father's huge hands in his small ones. "No!" Waukewa cried. "I won't let you!"

His father lifted Waukewa high into the air and burst into laughter. "Look at the brazen little warrior I have raised, Mother!" he said.

Then he agreed to let his son keep the eagle until it could fly again. "Then you must set it free," he said.

Many moons passed as Waukewa cared for the eagle. The bird grew stronger each day, as did their friendship. Finally the eagle was well enough to fly.

* *

Sadly the boy told his friend good-bye and raised him into the air. "Go, Little Eagle," Waukewa said. "The sky is your home—not my lodge."

The eagle soared in great swooping circles across the sky. And although the bird tried to come back to Waukewa several times, the boy shooed it away. Finally it disappeared into the clouds.

The eagle was gone, and so was summer. Fall and winter came and went. Then it was spring. Father and son, each in his own canoe, set out to hunt salmon. This time Waukewa decided to go to the high falls where the fish were abundant, even though his father had warned him of the dangerous current.

Waukewa waited until his father followed a fork in the river. Then he paddled to the high falls.

Unfortunately the boy was so busy catching fish he did not notice that his canoe was caught in the swift current. Soon the fragile boat was tossed by the rushing water against the perilous rocks. The canoe was out of control and was being swept toward the roaring falls ahead.

Certain that he was doomed, Waukewa began a chant to the Great Spirit. As he did, a shadow fell over the canoe. Waukewa looked up into the eyes of an eagle—his eagle. The boy stood up in the canoe as the bird swooped toward him. Just as the canoe was washed over the falls, Waukewa reached up and grabbed the eagle's legs.

Wings flapping wildly, the eagle fought its way out of the falls. Waukewa clung to its legs until the exhausted bird was able to land on a sandbar.

Still trembling at his close call, Waukewa stroked the bird's wet feathers. The eagle responded by nuzzling the boy's hand. Then, as suddenly as it appeared, the eagle soared into the sky with a cry of farewell.

"Yes, Little Eagle," said Waukewa, "now we are even."

When Plato closed the book, Aurora said, "What a story! Don't birds make the very best friends?"

"I guess friendships aren't like instant cocoa," Annie said to Plato. "They take time to make. But how do you know if a friend is going to be a true friend?"

"Good question," said Plato, pulling weeds from a patch of wildflowers. Aurora followed Plato, picking up the weeds in her beak and carrying them away.

"The important part of being a friend are the virtues each person brings to the friendship," Plato continued. "Even if it's just a helping beak."

"You mean like courage and loyalty," said Zach, remembering Waukewa's courage in standing up to his father, and the eagle's loyalty to the boy who had saved its life.

Annie realized all Sarah had wanted was the canoe. "She didn't care about me at all," Annie said.

Just then Sock accidentally stepped into one of Ari's holes. He started to sink, waving frantically. Ari quickly grabbed Sock's paws, and held tight until Plato arrived.

"Friendship also means knowing when a friend is in trouble," said Plato, pulling Sock out of the hole.

"Thanks, guys. You saved my life," said Sock.

"You're welcome, Sock," said Plato, "but it was something anyone would do for a friend."

"Just like the eagle," said Aurora, pulling some grass off Sock's ear. "It was there when Waukewa needed help."

"Maybe some day I'll have a *real* friend like Waukewa," said Annie.

"Well," Zach said to Annie, "I'm not a great hunter or anything . . . but would you consider going canoeing with me?"

"Are you sure you don't mind being seen in a leaky old canoe?" Annie joked.

"Hey, I'm great at bailing out," said Zach. "But not like Sarah!"

"It looks like Annie already has a good friend," said Ari.

"I just love happy endings," said Sock, resting his paw on Ari's shoulder. Unfortunately, the weight of Sock's paw caused Ari to sink down into the hole.

Annie and Zach smiled as Plato helped Sock pull Ari out of the hole.

When it was time for Annie to go home, Zach walked with her. On the way, they talked about the canoe trip. It sounded like so much fun, Annie almost forgot about Sarah.

The following Saturday the river was packed with canoes. It was a glorious day for canoeing. Shooting the rapids with Zach was one of the most exciting things Annie had ever done.

On the way home they passed Sarah and Ashley. The two girls never did get to the rapids. It turned out that neither of them knew how to handle a canoe.

At the end of the day Aurora circled above the river, and she heard Annie and Zach singing a song they had learned at Plato's Peak:

"Cherish friendships in your breast,

New is good, but old is best.

Make new friends, but keep the old;

Those are silver, these are gold."